Rose of Desire
The Novel

By

Anita Johnson Brown

ISBN 978-1-956010-50-3 (paperback)
ISBN 978-1-956010-51-0 (digital)

Rushmore Press LLC
1 800 460 9188
www.rushmorepress.com

Printed in the United States of America

PART 1

Anna Bella the Bored Housewife

More erotic romance from the files of Chris and Anita Brown.

Will the beautiful, thick, and sexy Anna Bella Errol be tempted to seek new pleasure or stay monogamous? Will she continue to be faithful or charmed to try the bittersweet taste of honey eroticism while her showbiz workaholic husband Manuel Errol's job keeps him on the road? This is a short story that will have you wanting and needing more.

The next short story will be honey eroticism (adult content), very erotic, romance. This is the teaser.

Rose of Desire the Novel* Anna Bella Errol

Anna Bella the Bored Housewife (all rights reserved). Adult content. Fiction.

Will beautiful Anna Bella Errol get so lonely and bored being a faithful wife, who is left alone craving for her husband or will she taste the temptation of having a secret love affair with a tall handsome stranger she meets at the coffee shop who strikes up a conversation while waiting in line to be served? Will coffee and donuts be the only things that get served, or will Anna Bella be offered something else sweet to taste while her famous husband is at his second home, on the road entertaining the world? Will someone else entertain Anna Bella's heart and her sexual desires or will this rose of desire stay true? Find out in the romance files of Chris and Anita Brown's adult content romance that is very intimate. Anna Bella the bored housewife is an intimate peril of seduction. On the fiction side of this story, the names have been changed to protect the innocent or the not-so-innocent to keep you guessing and your imagination running wild in this intimate fantasy that is based on reality. Curl up in bed and read it slowly so you can taste every bit of this story. It will surely whet your appetite for love and desire.

Anna Bella Errol sat by the phone. He still hadn't called. She missed him so much, though it wasn't anything new. His work kept him on the road most of the time. She inhaled, brushed her hands across her dresses, and walked to the window. Anna Bella was beautiful for her age. Any man would want her. They would even choose to die for her. At 5'4 inches tall, she's curvy, beautiful, intelligent, sexy, and stuck up, but if you got to know her and she chooses to have you in her life, you would meet one of the nicest and most lovable people in the world. You would think she had a master's degree in every subject that dealt with life. She gave good sound advice. It came from the heart as most of her choices did but she also spoke from her mind, and Manuel Errol her husband is one of the most famous men in show business. He was always an influence on Anna Bella's decisions. They were made for each other. They were inseparable.

Anna thought more and more about Errol—her husband is one of the most famous men in show business, always busy, always a mist in the wind, smiling at other women dancing and swooning them into a fantasy. All the while, Anna Bella waited at home for a phone call or text for any sign to show he loved her. After all, she went through torturous days and nights in the submission of proving her love for him. Other men would probably beat down her door just for a bit of a conversation and deluded attempts to talk her into bed but Anna Bella treated them nonchalantly. Men who flirted with her made her turn her head. They were appalling; they made her stomach boil in pain and had no appeal to her at all. She would never even think of losing herself to one of those run-of-the-mill bull pull-hitters who need another notch gathered on their belts. She would literally kill them if they even tried to come near her. The thought of having sex with a man you have no attraction to is like losing every part of your life, like having sex with the most horrifying creature and fighting for your life, almost like rape. It would be such a horrible experience and a reason to hate men when we need them so much. However, no woman should have to face that type of agony. As for Anna Bella, the strength of securing one's petal of desire and heart was a challenge for mankind. Only a certain type of man caught Anna Bella's eyes—Errol—he is and always will be the winner. Men were created to be kings and heads of the household, delete kingdoms, nations, and be leaders, have power and guidance, and influence others to be leaders. Why should women be the ones to rule the world? Just one showing of weakness shows the fidelity and mindset of a boy, not to mention the failure of him as a man. Men waited for the chance to take Anna from Errol. Did the thought ever cross her mind to cheat? Did the thought ever cross her mind that she is the prize, a precious jewel? It was Errol who is the love of her life. She thought about him when she woke up and before she went to bed, he was on her mind all the time, during the day until the middle of the night. And when she needed to make love, she thought about Errol. He was the only man she wanted to be with.

Anna's thoughts of Errol started to overpower her imagination. It created an impulse to run her hands all over her body. The small fan she had blowing in the corner of the room made her half-naked body tingle as she started to fantasize about her and Errol making love and the front of it. Then, she looked up from her fashion magazine, and through the window, she could see the neighbors making love. Anna Bella lingered her eyes on the couple and imagined it was her and Errol. This excited Anna Bella so much she felt herself get moist. Her vagina area started to respond and she needed to give in to the desire of touching herself, of spreading her perfect rose petals apart and caressing her rose. But damn, if only Mr. Errol were home. Anna got it from the chaise lounge throwing the magazine to the floor, her eyes still on the window. They were really getting into it now and her neighbor's hands moved across his partner's body like an artist creating a sculpture. Anna Bella walked away from the window and went to the lonely bedroom. She looked up at the wall of the photo of Errol and herself hanging there, taunting her, teasing her, making her miss him even more. He was away so much and as the old saying goes, all men cheat! That's a disappointment. Well, instead of money, the precious vagina should be the root of man's evil and the deception to make him ruin and even lose his life. Anna smiled, "We women have the power to turn heads and to chop them off, causing a man to lose everything. It's funny how the term pussy whipped should be a legal term defined in the dictionary as the cause of ending a relationship. The vagina can control minds, rule the world, and even take down the most powerful leaders. The vagina, the precious birth canal, is where man came from and where he wants to return and we oblige to him by giving in, by submitting to him, but some of us without the respect or pride of being a woman. The most beautiful specimen created on earth is defined as a woman but a man's urge to return to the soft puddle of the wet tasty cave surrounding him and making him feel safe is the weakness of his life, his paradise. Men cheat with games and determination and we choose to love them with emotion and from the depths of our hearts."

Through the window, she could see the neighbors making love. This excited Anna Bella. She felt herself get moist. Damn, if only Mr. Errol were home. Anna walked away from the window and took her vibrator out of the bedroom drawer. She called her husband by his last name, Mr. Errol. Anna had used the toy this morning. It was still shiny with her juices. The way she pushed it in and out of her made her scream out Errol's name. She masturbated for an hour and was about to start again.

Anna unwrapped the plastic from around the long rubbery vibrator. The head of it reminded her of Errol. She sat down to watch the neighbors. They were doing it doggy style. You could see his penis going in and out of her. The woman threw her head back, her mouth was open, and she pushes with every stroke to meet him.

Anna thought of Errol. She thought they were both the ingredients to a special recipe of love. She never thought of any other man since their marriage. Anna Bella rubbed her hand up and down the vibrator and tucked it inside the plastic. It was still moist. Her morning escapade made her think of Errol more and more. She loved making him fall under her spell. He was her sex toy. He obeyed her every command. Her thoughts of Errol took over and Anna Bella wanted him to join her. She wanted him to hear her moan his name and to make him explode and drained completely.

Anna picked up her cellphone and dialed. She whispered, "Errol, please answer." She whispered his name as she touched herself gently. She moaned his name as she listened to the phone ring. She screamed his name especially when he was inside her, drilling her oil well, making her overflow. Anna always made Errol cry out her name. The phone kept ringing; there was no answer. She clicked the end of the call button and sat down on the bed. She was so damn lonely. She felt deserted a bit, lifeless, except for the craving between her legs. Anna walked to the window. She was frustrated. She wanted Errol to cover and love her. She was the only one he loved. Supposedly, she wanted to feel him deep inside her, the man she loves and desires. Anna was mad because there was no answer. She thought to herself, "I will bite my tongue. I'm tortured and I've been tortured long enough." Anna laid down on the floor in the living room in front of the window and made self-love until she was sore, then again, in the shower she was squirting, thinking of Errol, and calling his name. If only he had been able to watch her touch herself; thinking of him made her feel good inside. Anna Bella took another shower to take the edge off. Here she was, she thought, while drying off with her favorite pink soft fluffy towel. The softness of the towel only put her in the mood again for her husband Errol. She wanted to make love to him in the middle of the bathroom floor where they had made love on that same pink towel before he left to go on the road. Anna went to the bedroom then laid across the bed looking at Errol's picture again. Anna thought to herself, "I can lay here or I can take a stroll. Maybe I'll buy a puppy or pick up some groceries. Maybe go to a movie. Hopefully, no strangers will be playing with himself at the movies. Enough of that." The site she endured as a teenager was appalling—men masturbating while she and her friends sat and laughed at them. Not that Anna Bella didn't like porn, she did, but with Errol.

Brand-Chris and Anita Brown

Anna Bella the Beginning

Anna Bella the Beginning, from the files of Chris and Anita Brown (all rights reserved), adult content, non-fiction, private files released, erotic, smooth drama I, we, me, and you tell the story in narrative.

Anabella got home late from her stroll, she didn't buy any puppies; she picked up a few groceries and magazines. Errol's face was on the front of one of them. Anna walked to the bathroom, washed her face and hands, and put her groceries up. She could still feel the heat of the sun. It warmed her body. Anabella walked back to the living room and sat down. The rays from the sun were still shining in the living room window. She loved the way the heat felt against her body. She picked up her cellphone to look through her social media. That's what most people do when they don't have much of social life and when loneliness kicks in and stabs them in the gut. She sat there thumbing through the pages. It was like her world had fallen apart. She was so bored and lonely it seemed like there was a pattern in her life where she would go years without any male contact. This was not the first time in-between boyfriends. It would be six years before she would find a permanent mate. Either no one would be interested or she would not be interested in them. Anna Bella was picky about friends and especially about the men in her life. Even when growing up, she stayed isolated from people who didn't fit in her life. She hated **** starters, troublemakers, and just plain ********. Anna Bella's parents took very good care of her and her brother. They had the best of everything that they didn't know what poor was and never found out until Anna Bella was grown. She got her first job at an upscale store in Los Angeles Bullock's Wilshire. Anna Bella graduated from a business college with a degree in business management. From college, all the things around her from caviar to name brands, everything—Anna Bella always had expensive tastes and dress very well. Her father worked for the city for twenty-four years and her mother was a housewife. Anna Bella's father was very strict and did not allow her to date boys or even think about them. Her family was the stuck-up family in that neighborhood as most kids there came from single-family homes or mothers who changed their boyfriends like underwear. Anna Bella pushed some of her thoughts away and looked at her page again. She saw a pic of Chris Brown and posted it. What a handsome guy, young and sexy. He looked very respectful and charming and although Anna Bella knew she was older than him, she developed a crush on the young talented musician-entertainer, singer-songwriter artist and she could tell he was a master of almost everything. Is he also a master at love? She didn't know out until years later. Anna relaxed in her chair. It was getting dark outside and so was her soul. Her heart was broken too many times by boys, the ones who pushed themselves in her life which consisted of coworkers and friends, and the death of loved ones. For the most part of Anna's life, the only things in her life were heartache and pain, but the puzzle remains unsolved— why was she still a woman who went without sex for a series of six years and without someone to love her? The sad part is her life was broken. Anna is a sexy, curvy, alluring woman with great morals and standards. She wasted so much time in isolation from the outside world wishing she could expand her wings and let the world know she did exist. She has so much to offer the world. Her imagination for writing is the reality in which she exists. Her ultimate passion is writing. If only someone would notice that she is real and not just the vivid imagination of those who wish to know her. She is a real woman who is so damn special that God would bless her with someone who is also designed just for her—a man unavailable to other women because they are a match made in heaven. Anna would love to travel and experience new things, learn about other cultures, taste different delectable delights, and clean her tongue palate with the sherbet of reality instead of just dreaming about it. She would love to lay on the beach with ice cold lemonade and watch the children play, or look and oversee the man she loves sitting next to her with his headphones on listening to music or riding with her. This would be an adventure in itself. With her laptop on her lap and a lawn chair, they would be writing a new book and several would capture the hearts of millions from children to adults. She prays one day that someone will notice her existence and they will do the things that she has done with no other man, like falling deeply in love. Anna got up and walked to the kitchen to fix dinner. She had to be on the phone at 8:00 PM. Believe it or not, she made her living talking to lonely, unsatisfied men who needed someone to share their feelings with. Why they couldn't talk to their wives was a mystery. Why they couldn't share their thoughts, desires, secrets, and needs with the women or men they have fallen in love with was indeed a mystery to the men who made it a point to call her like clockwork either every week or every day. There was always someone to talk to in her job, and she isn't doing this to escape by phone or out of the need of their attention. She made good money opening offices in Las Vegas, Los Angeles, and visiting an office opened in Detroit. Not to be racist or a bigot, she prefers to be around the people that would give her an opportunity to become something other than a lazy female doing nothing. Never look a gift rabbit in the mouth. That phone erratic communications operator job led her to a position as office supervisor district manager and stockholder in the company but before that, Anna stayed in a band for years. Phyllis's brother Lorenzo Patterson was also a member of N.W.A. The group N.W.A would usually be in the living room discussing the music business and gigs. We all traveled one day to an NWA's gig in Los Angeles. Phyllis and Anna were in the car. An N.W.A was in the truck in the back. People were blowing their horns and hanging out their windows and just come to think of it, this was before they made their millions. Gigs were how shows are called back in the day. Anna Bella was one of the ladies in the band called Jupiter featuring Ladies of Love. Anna was the lead singer and Dee Dee and Linda sang background. Anna remembers the song she had. Mark the band leader sang it. It was a love song and a beautiful one. Mark and Anna Bella's relationship was purely platonic but when they sang that song together, they looked like real lovers. Mark was dating Tela at the time. Anna play sister and best friend. Back in the day, we used to always go to a club where they saw a band called Custom Made. Anna liked a guy named Bryant Mclemore and Tela was really in love with Byron Blue. No worries, we never did a thing. Mark later dated Phyllis. The members of the Jupiter band were Mark, Butch, Roosevelt, and Donald. I hope you guys are doing great. I didn't miss anybody, and if I did, it wasn't intentional. Anna Bella is still friends with Mark and his brothers, Tony and Dario, doing her days and the band. Anna Bella could belt out Anita Baker's and Chaka Khan's songs like an angel with a voice so smooth and sweet, breaking those crystal champagne glasses with her soprano voice, although she sang alto in her high school choir while Ricky Minor played piano who later went on to work for Whitney Houston. Anna performed at the patriotic hall with the Jupiter band astonishing the audience with their standing ovation. The Jupiter band members later left in pursuit of other business opportunities. Mark is still a great musician playing around the world with his band The Full Flava Kings.

I need to call in to see if Mark and Calvin Broadus-Snoop ever did that song together. Mark always wanted to work with him. Anna took a break from thinking about the past. She gave up singing, a career that she always wanted to have. She loved music. She could hear the notes so clearly in a song it seemed like music was made just for her. She gave up her career due to domestic violence and was replaced by a band member's lover during the victimization of domestic violence. Her manager, Mark's mom Pat, came to her rescue. She became part of their family. If Anna Bella's father knew she was being beaten while he was doing his inventory at Johnson cleaners on Compton Ave., he would have spent the rest of his life in prison defending his daughter. Anna hid in her room; she would go to Pat's home when she was beaten. Her face was unrecognizable. Anna Bella is no stranger to domestic violence of any type—emotional, physical, financial, religious, and more but through it all, she's a great woman becoming a domestic violence advocate. Later on, the things a partner will do to keep you in the clutches of his insecurity, if you only knew, if you dare leave a person with violent behavior, they would realize they are the piece of **** they always knew they were.

Anna married because she was lonely due to the death of her mother. This man was younger than Anna Bella who continued to beat her viciously, making it impossible for her to continue her lifelong dream as a singer or anything else. She made the mistake of getting married at a young age because she wanted someone to hold her and take her away from the mental and physical anguish. Later, she escaped the clutches of this person better known as the creature and made a new life. Anna became a CNA nurse in Las Vegas and Los Angeles. Anna continued to work as an exotic communications operator before earning a degree in business management. She also was the music manager with a few clients who used to perform at the Roosevelt Hotel in Hollywood. She was an executive producer in a film called Recycled Lives written by Paul Haas. She owned a company called Illusions Unlimited Company, Maximum Entertainment, and another management company Bonafide Entertainment with her business partner Vince. Later on, Anna Bella was introduced to Katt Williams by her assistant Ariana. Anna Bella and Katt Williams managed in a business deal so the people who Anna Bella managed could perform and do shows. A few of the people she managed were Shaun Price, Charles Mathers, T Marvin, Williams, Sean, and David, and then she gained a new business partner by the name of Kelvin Jiles. Kathleen managed the entertainment department at the Hollywood Park casino; much respect to Katt for giving Anna Bella's music performers a chance to evolve. Anna Bella met Rodney Perry and a few other comedians who were making their way to start him. Anna Bella wrote a few scripts—The Con and the Mumseys and a few others later on. With Anna Bella's knowledge and skills that she learned over the years, she was employed at a bank doing home loans, verifying client signatures, and navigating through famous people's property debts, gains, and losses. There, information is private; it always will be. She loved working at a well-known car dealership as a salesperson where she met Damu, a musician, and they became close friends. He was also the producer of a documentary short film about Anna Bella and now owns a photography studio. The men and the receptionist at the dealership in Culver City were nice to Anna. She was greeted with a smile. She also worked in a property management and phone company as a coach and assistant supervisor. There were just a few of the major positions she held and now a writer, she wanted to be as a child and is still interested in photography. Anna Bella will release a photo book later this year of never-seen photos of Chris Brown and his family members. Anna grew up knowing she would make the choices in life about who becomes a part of her world and although the legitimate men she met had jobs and maybe even goals, she will always remember they treated her like ****. They made her life a living hell. She would never let any ******* come into her life to destroy her again, rich or poor, and to this day, she is cautious of who wins her trust. She thought she would not find love until she met him, the man who won her heart, and she falls in love with him.

Anna Bella got up from her comfortable brown leather chair after thinking about some of her past accomplishments. She needed to dust off some of the memory, especially the part that hurt her the most, and fixed dinner. She returned to her favorite chair. She fried chicken, made rice pilaf, and roasted asparagus. Anna loves the taste of fine cuisine. She has expensive taste buds and has tasted some of the finest dishes cooked by some of the best chefs when working for Communa Phone Incorporated. She experienced the nub hub of hanging with millionaires. Her boss was one and they became very close friends, sharing secrets, eating expensive dinners, shopping, traveling, and more. Anna Bella learned a lot from Darlene who was one of the people she felt comfortable with. Once you make a true friendship with a person, they become hard to replace. Let's just say there may never be a female friend in her life like Darlene again. It may seem strange but over the years, Anna Bella found it more appealing to be friends with men rather than women until she met Diane and they became friends which turned into a business relationship. My friendship with men, I didn't date or it was strictly platonic, no sexual or intimate contact. We could talk to each other about anything and the men weren't messy or jealous of Anna Bella and if they had anything bad to say, she would never know. These days, Anna Bella would prefer to be friends with the man she loves. Anna Bella also had a few friends who were bisexual and same sexual. She finished eating and set her plate on the coffee table. She heard footsteps by the window and decided to close it. She was never friendly with her neighbors. Anna Bella washed a few dishes in the sink and turned to her chair to watch her favorite show. After that, she went to the bathroom to run a nice, hot bubble bath, being very attracted to the sensual smells and warm water touching her skin. She couldn't wait to soak in the tub. She undressed in her bedroom, laid her clothes across the bed, walked to the bathroom, and a thought ran across her mind as she looked at herself in a mirror on the way to the bathroom. Why wasn't she dating anymore? Anna Bella remembered having a friend she used to talk to by the name of Q. They talked every night, but he would just keep on talking about his girlfriend and how she was cheating on him. That was terrible. He seemed like such a nice guy and she felt so relaxed talking to him but when Anna Bella found a boyfriend who she was interested in, she told him she couldn't talk to him anymore. He seemed heartbroken and so did Anna Bella. That was a mistake. What's puzzling is that he never told her his real name. That's the sad part. Anyway, Anna Bella broke up with her boyfriend Don after six years and it was six years more before she dated anyone else.

Anna started to drown in the thoughts of her past so she put her foot in the tub to test the water. The temperature was just right. She sat in the tub. The smell of lavender and roses engulfed her nostrils, sending her into a state of relaxation. She braced her naked body against the back of the tub, reached over for a few candles, and struck one of the long matchsticks on the side of the tub. The water was so hot. Anna Bella's body temperature started to rise. She thought about the fantasy she had when she was lonely and she needed to have an orgasm. It's about a girl wanting to be tied up while she is standing and made love to slowly, very slowly, because she had never had an orgasm before. And a gentleman walks in the room. The room is dark and all you can see is the oiled-up body of a female. She's waiting and breathing hard. As he approaches her, she looks up at him and you can see her stomach muscles contracting. He walks up to her and looks her in the eyes. He touches her only with his tongue, running his tongue all over her lips, kissing her, and tasting her tongue. Her body starts to shiver, then his finger moves to that intimate spot, and she is mesmerized by his touch. She is helpless. Well, he suggested tasting and touching every part of her body leaving her screaming in ecstasy. He leaves her there but unties the satin sash from around her wrist. She lays down on the bed next to where she was tied up to a pole, then she starts to dance for him and he is enchanted by the way her body moves.

Anna dried off and went to her bedroom. The dimness of the light and the romantic music playing in the background reminded her of how she ached inside. She threw herself on the bed and fell asleep.

If you like Anna Bella, keep your eyes out for book three, and thanks to those celebs who follow on social media, the hubby Christopher Maurice Brown, Jaceyon Taylor, Calvin Broadus, O'Shea Jackson, Lorenzo Patterson, a whole lot more, and a few disc jockeys who followed me. One chose to have no affiliation but hey, here's a smile, we never dated, so nobody knows who you are. So, put your wife or girlfriend's mind at rest, but I wish you luck and success.

Anna Bella in the series book four, the Erotic Housewife. A non-fiction story with a small twist of fiction to protect the innocent and not-so-innocent. Novel by Anita Johnson Brown/Anita Brown. Continues with Anna Bella opening the letter she and Errol composed on their honeymoon.

Soft and Beautiful, My Intimate Rose of Desire By Anita Johnson-Brown— Inspired by Chris Brown*

A burning rose of desire is the way you light my fire. It ignites my burning flame to a forever-lasting passion only for you. Your touch and everlasting vibe ignite my soul and make me drip like candle wax, so warm and soft. The liquid pours down my breast and trickles around my belly button. As a whiff of your perfume cascades in the memory of my rose of desire, I wish to taste his secret and he desires to manipulate mine. Gentle strokes of desire and rose petals float inside the ocean of love as we lay submerged in our own passion. She lights every inch of my love wand and the softness of her voice whispers in my ear. I began to melt from the heat of her delicate touch. Her hands wander over my body to find every inch of weakness, seducing and satisfying me. She delights in the loyal pleasures of craving only me and I fill her rose petal with every inch of me. My sweet rose of desire touches my ear with her most gentle expression and whispers, "Love more." She is mine, my pretty, gorgeous, lovely rose of desire, pleasing and immersing me with waves of indulgence, the only love I desire. I captivate his mind, body, and soul with love as I sip slowly, drinking his love potion, spellbinding me as we gaze at the red moon. Together, we want to be in a timeless capsule of each other, and above any other, I long to curb his appetite from any other distraction, and he has the compulsion to show me perfect love as we commit to fulfilling each other's every need. I am his oxygen and he is my air. We are each other's heart's desire. From his heart to my heart, our love beads lather and pours like rain. Drops of her morning dew fall against my skin. It smells so sweet as it penetrates my nostrils and carries me into a deeper trance of pure seduction. With her gentle and smooth touch, her caramel skin is plush and lovely. My strong heart weakens as she overdoses me with her love and liquid honey. I can't get enough of her and she begs for all of me. She became my need to thrive and I need her to survive. We are not shallow or dense but a knot of love made for each other. We are God's plan of two lovers combined as one just as the stars are in the sky and the moon sits above our heads. The sun rises. It lights our way and the beauty of an evening sunset gives us the notion to plunge into a timeless reality. We hold the hands of matrimony as a token of our everlasting love. Like the petals of a flower, I will catch you when you fall. I will gather the branches and twigs to build you an eternity. Just as there are heaven and earth, you are my heaven on earth. We make a language of melodies, flowing and expressing just some of the love I feel for you. My love for you can fill an eternity and build a lifetime of happiness. You are my rose of desire. You are my heaven on earth. You light the torch of my desire and guide me into a lifetime of brightness as I have never known. It amazes me how well we convey our love. To know and feel you inside out is my only desire. Our thoughts seem to find a way to each other when we are away from one another. It's as if the third eye of vision travels to unite us. Like nature intended, we come together like a blooming rose. Not a day goes by when I don't feel the need to be next to you, holding and feeling your body next to mine. You are my one and only rose of desire. I am on the verge of explosive love, spreading petals of love, and indulging in the angelic smell of roses. Your precious desires and thoughts are no longer just a mere dream. You have made a step into reality, my one and only rose of desire.

Chris and Anita Brown

(via Chris and Anita Brown) I LOVE YOU

Indio season

Rose of Desire and Heaven on Earth collide for everlasting love. Our next story is called Easy Rider.

His flow and sounds were magic. Her vibe was the most tempting he would ever taste. They rode off into the sunset to a love life that would last forever. Meet Chris Brown and Anita Brown in Easy Rider, coming soon to the After Dark files. Only by Chris and Anita Brown.

Easy Rider

Chris drove up to his estate. The hum of his motorcycle sounded loudly as he took the curb that leads to his garage. The sun was about to set. The sky was clear and the day had been beautiful. He took his phone out to look at her number and photo. He put the phone back in his jacket pocket and reached on the side of his bike to tap the clicker, but he remembered he left it on the kitchen counter. They were remodeling the front entry where he usually drove in. Chris parked against the side of the garage. He enjoyed the ride so much. As he was proceeding down the highway, he took the freeway, then a shortcut along the street until he got to Vine. He hadn't been this way in a long time to Hollywood. He drove down the Vine to Hancock Park. As he looked on the right at the Hancock Country Club which he had not been to in a long time and passed Beverly Boulevard on the left, he noticed they were doing construction on a commercial property. As he drove alone, his mind wandered to the female he saw at the gym. She is thick. I know her body is soft. I never had a thick one before. This could be the beginning of a meaningful situation. A sexy, older, and totally beautiful brown-skinned, brown-eyed queen, her walk made men turn to look at her, a real woman from head to toe. And I do mean woman. She commanded attention when she walked into a room. I went a few times just to see her. I didn't know a woman could have this effect on me. His mind went back to the traffic ahead. Before he knew it, he was heading toward Wilshire Blvd. He made a right at the light and drove down Crenshaw, maintaining the speed limit. He thought about how fate brought them together. Just thinking about her made his 6-foot 1-inch tall frame weak with desire. He wondered if she was as laid back as she seemed, but wild in other ways. He remembered the gym. Anita crossed his mind again. He went a few more times but didn't see her. That was disappointing and she's been on his mind all the time. Is this what it's like to have an attachment to a female? And he had had many—some a waste of time, some for sex, and some for show, more like a trophy with no engraving—but none like her. Chris wanted to know her, touch her, spend time with her, and talk to her. She intrigued him. He loved the way she smelled even after exercising. Her perfume was intoxicating. Chris loved Los Angeles. There was always something to do. He rode until he reached Santa Monica. He parked on Appian Way in Lot 1 North, got off his bike, locked and chained it, walked along the pier, and stopped at Pacific Park World for chicken tacos. They have a world championship taco-eating contest. People come from everywhere around the world to eat tons of tacos and cheer each other on. It's a big deal and the prize is over 4500.00 bucks. The champion takes half of the winnings, but for Chris, there would be no contest for him today, just a quick bite before he walked along the pier. If he could see her, it would be fate, more like heaven on earth.

Chris was about to take another bite of his taco when he looked to his left. His nose took in a whiff of perfume. The scent made him think of her immediately. The intoxicating sweet smell stopped him from chewing. He couldn't take another bite or swallow. When he took a second look, it was her, the beauty from the gym. He stared at her. She turned around and caught his eye. She smiled. He wondered what her name was. He held his head down and tried to swallow. It seemed as if the taco was stuck in his throat. Chris took a sip from his drink. He finally managed to swallow his food down. He eyed her between bites. He looked down again and said, "Down, boy" (meaning the bulge in his pants). She looked at him again before taking a seat. The waiter came over to take her order. A chicken taco plate with the works was what she ordered with pink lemonade. She crossed her legs and pulled a book out of her purse. She opened it to the middle part of the book, looked up, and caught my eye. That was my queue. I couldn't take my eyes off her. I decided to get up and ask her if I could join her.

Chris walked over to Anita. She looked up and uncrossed her legs. She immediately said hello to him and asked if he would like to join her. Chris said, "Yeah. Thanks for asking. Just what I had in mind." Anita handed him the menu. I guess another taco wouldn't be a bad idea. "I'm Chris, and you are?" She said, "I'm Anita, nice to meet you. I saw you at the gym. I was on the cardio machine walking for an hour, trying to pick up my pace to run/jog on it. You spoke to me when I was leaving. Sorry, I was walking by in a hurry. I usually don't talk to guys unless I know them more but I really didn't hear you until I passed by you. Sorry about that." She looked deep into his eyes. "I recognized you when I walked in and thought to myself this is fate and I promised I wouldn't miss out on speaking to you." Chris was surprised but got more comfortable. The waiter walked over to where Chris was sitting and cleared the table. He brought Chris a coke and Anita's lemonade to the table where Anita and Chris were sitting together. The waiter picked up the menu, smiled at Chris, and nodded his head. "Another?" He answered yes. After they both were served, they ate and eyed each other. They were so fascinated with each other that no words needed to be spoken at the time and Christopher started the conversation with the usual—single, children, where do you work? Do you work tomorrow? Have your own home or rent? What do you do? She answered, "I live around the corner. A long corner, maybe twenty minutes from here. You should come by later or whenever you are free. Tonight would be great. We can relax, talk some more, get to know each other." She didn't ask Chris any questions and instead handed him her card and picked up the check. "This one's on me. Nice meeting you. Call me!" He kind of looked at her in a questionable way. Chris threw some cash on the table. Anita turned to look at Chris, "That can be the tip since you already paid for your first meal. This is my treat. I promise you can and will, in fact, pay the next time. If you have nothing to do, stop by later. My address is on the card. I work from home." Chris was speechless, and he wanted to get to know her better, as a matter of fact. Before she left, she asked for a hug. He stood up and hugged her. It felt good and stimulating. He sort of laughed and said, "How far do you live from here?" She said, "About twenty minutes, not far. Stop by, Mr. Chris Brown. I've been a fan for years. Maybe I can show you my CB photo album and a book I'm writing." She walked out. He wondered if she was easy and just to ease his mind, Anita turned around and said, "No, I'm not easy, Chris. Don't get the wrong idea. I've been celibate for 6 years. It would be nice to get to know you better. I think we have a lot in common. I know you won't be disappointed." She turned and left. He looked at her card and sat back down at the table. When the waiter came over, he asked, "How often does—" The waiter interrupted, "Anita!" He said, "Yes, how often she comes in here?" "She comes a few times a week; sometimes with her laptop. I think she is a writer, always comes alone." He asked the waiter to tab the cash for her. Chris asked Justin the waiter, "Do you know her personally?" Justin said, "Not really. She's quiet and not too social, very picky. I'm just assuming because she travels solo, she keeps to herself." Chris looked at his watch and left the restaurant. He walked around the pier for an hour. When he started walking toward his motorcycle, he took out her card. He knew the area well. He took out his cell and dialed her number but as he got closer to his bike, he saw a single rose laid across his seat. Holding it, there was a piece of small tape and a notecard that had her name across it—Anita. He thought this is a different one. He finished dialing the number. Anita answered, "Hello, Christopher, I see you got my rose. Are you on your way?" Chris laughed and coughed a little, "Ahh! Yes, I guess so." She asked Chris if he would like anything prepared for him or anything special he would like to do. He said, "No, if so, I'll bring it with me." Anita said, "Okay, see you when you get here."

Anita got home, sat in the car for a minute, and laid her head back on the headrest. "Hmmm. I wonder if I was too fresh with him. I hope not." She reached for her laptop and the tall lemonade she had in the cup holder got out of the car. She set her things down on the chair next to the door, opened it, and as soon as it was inside, she flipped the light switch on and went to the kitchen. Anita placed the laptop and the lemonade on the table. She went to the bathroom, ran a bath, walked in her bedroom, took her jacket off, hung it up in the closet, went back into the kitchen, put the lemonade in the freezer, kicked her shoes off next to the kitchen table, and turned her laptop on. The title of the book was:

Players in the Ghetto, Deception, Lies, and Bedroom Scandal (all rights reserved). This will be the next book Chris and I write.

(Thou shall not sleep with thy neighbor's wife or husband.)

She was almost finished with the book. It was written primarily about the men and women who cheated as a game or hobby. Disgusting was too good of a word for spreading your body around like a male whore, or as somebody once said for females, a Babylon whore. My own insert is just a damn female version of Satan or a female demon in disguise, diminishing our population with sexual disease. Among other things such as broken marriages, friendships, partnerships, and more, you must read the book to enjoy the dirty details.

Anita closed the laptop. She was waiting on Chris to come. She went straight to the bathroom and undressed. The silk blouse she was wearing was sticking to her body. She unbuttoned it and placed it across the chair. She unzipped her skirt on the side and let it drop to the floor. She put one foot in the tub to test the water. It was really warm, just the way she liked it. She removed the white-laced panties and bra. She stood naked in the bathroom, adoring herself, wondering why she hadn't dated anyone in so many years. She thought about Chris as she stepped into the tub and started to wash her body. She felt excited. Seeing him at the beach diner was a dream come true. She dreamed of him on all those lonely long nights. After seeing him at the gym and saying hello, she was mesmerized by his smile, the way he walked, and the way he was direct with what he said. She watched him on the cardio machine at the gym and their stride matched each other. She wondered what it would be like to ride him, to mount his body, and feel how hard he would be when she would slowly slide him between her legs and look in his eyes. Anita wanted to tighten her muscles around him and feel Chris inside of her for hours. She wanted to spread whip cream on his body and lick it off. Her desires went deep; she wanted to insert a strawberry halfway inside her after she dipped it in whip cream and let Chris taste it while she took his manhood in her hands, stroking it up and down with just a small piece of chipped ice in her mouth, taking just the head of his penis in her mouth and teasing it, then taking a bite of something warm to tease him even more. And now he was on his way to her, but she would not engage in wonderful lovemaking tonight. No, not yet, he would have to wait and so would she. Anita wanted to know every inch of him mentally and physically, everything. She wanted Chris as her man and she was determined to get him. Anita thought, "Damn, I haven't been attracted to any man in years but he has been on my mind for so damn long I refuse to let him go. I hope he feels the same."

Chris got on his bike then took a second look at the rose Anita left on his bike. He took the petals off the rose and put them in his pocket, letting the stem of the rose fall to the sand. He looked up at the sky and said, "Lord, what am I in store for? This woman has my complete interest, but I think I will take my time with her, proceed slow, get to know her." She has more to offer than just sex, even though he had thought about her on nights when he was in the studio. Writing songs, he wanted to make love to her, not just screw her brains out. It would be nice to get to know her inside out, and he would, that was a promise. He would without a doubt.

Anita soaked in the tub until she felt her skin tingle from the softness of the water and Chanel bath suds and oil. She then washed every part of her body in a delicate manner making sure the good-smelling scent stayed on her body. The clock on the wall in the bathroom said 7:30 PM. She was waiting for Chris to come, excited and ready to see him again.

I stepped out of the tub and got my towel. I could still smell the delicate scent on my body. That bath felt wonderful, my body felt soft and warm, I used a small amount of body spray, as I didn't want to smell too strong. Wrapping the towel around my body, I walked back into the bedroom. My bed looked so good I could have stretched out on the bed and slept all night, but the anticipation of the man I dreamed of and yearned for desired and needed more ways than one. Chris Brown was on his way to me, something I had prayed for, and hoped he felt the same way. I went to the kitchen and made a cheese and veggie platter, chilled some wine, and made chicken tacos. I put everything in the warmer to make sure it was nice and hot for him. I didn't really know if he wanted anything else since we had just dined hours ago but it would be ready if we wanted to have something to munch later that night. I made sure to have all the sides ready.

Anita dressed in jeans and a tight-fitting green dressy blouse with medium green pumps. She pulled her hair up with a green band around her head and chose medium-sized gold earrings with the necklace to match. The blouse wasn't too low, but low enough to wonder what was hiding inside the blouse. The accent of the necklace made her neckline look great. After getting dressed, Anita walked around the house to make sure everything was neat and tidy. She went to her studio and took the Chris Brown photo album with her and the partial manuscript, which was almost finished to the living room. She had to add maybe sixteen more pages, and it would be finished. She wondered what he would think about the title. He would probably laugh. The thought of Chris laughing made her smile. She wanted to impress him. She knew he painted and had bought one of his paintings. It hung on the living room wall. It made her home look fascinating. She loves wall art, the expensive kind with nice frames. She paid a pretty penny to have the painting framed. She had more in her studio. Just two of them, she wondered if he liked to go to the Art Museum.

Chris took in the view as he rode his chopper to meet up with Anita. He couldn't get over the thought that she had left a single rose on his bike. He reached in his pocket and felt the rose petals. He put one up to his nose. He would put them in a vase for her and make rose water. He knew she liked to smell good. Her perfume was just intoxicating. It stirred more than his soul and just the thought of getting to know her inside out was enough to drive him wild. He wanted to hug her again. Damn! Her body felt so damn soft, and she smelled so good. It brought back the entire memory of when he hugged Anita before she left the beach. He kissed her on the cheek; he couldn't resist. Chris never met a woman that felt that good. He felt every part of her body, her skin was so soft and warm. Her breast against his chest, she pressed her body into him and they held each other for a while. She pulled away and held her head down. She was getting wet. It made him wonder more about her. When she pulled away, her breast slid across his chest, and she stood there for a moment and looked deep into his eyes. Maybe she felt his body respond to hers and thought she might not want to seem too eager and he was okay with that. After all, they wanted to get to know each other. She was a writer so was he, and Anita had more to offer than what was between her legs. Her vibe mixed with his, the thrill of getting to know her would be like getting high, floating on a cloud without the use of drugs. Knowing that you want someone and they want you back is a real blessing, especially if the person is worth it, and the wait. Chris wondered if they would make it through the night without tearing each other's clothing off. Chris turned down her street. She lived in a nice area. He saw her car in the driveway.

When Anita heard his bike in front of her house, she used the clicker to open the gate. He looked up at her door and thought, well, here goes. Chris drove the bike in the yard and looked around. He knew she lived alone because her car was dusty. Chris got off his bike. He noticed her coming to the door. She had changed clothes and was looking delicious. He could smell her from the driveway. She walked out on the porch and looked at him with a smile. "Hello, Mr. Brown," she said. "Why so formal, Anita?" She responded with her soft, sexy voice, "I just wanted to call you Mr. Brown. I'm sure there will be other occasions you will love when I call you Mr. Brown." He laughed, and she's a flirt. He said, "Keep talking like that and you might have to prove it." They lingered at each other. She asked him to come in, looked back at Chris, then took his hand and said, "I can prove more than you know." When Chris got inside, he looked around at her place. He pointed to the painting on the wall, "I don't believe you have that. That's one of my favorites, damn!" He thought, "I can't wait to see what else she has." Anita told Chris that was one of her favorites. "Have a seat. Are you hungry? Or can I get you a drink or something else? I know you smoke! I don't indulge, but you are more than welcome to make yourself at home." Chris sat on the couch next to Anita. She looked good to him. He laid his head on the back of the couch. She did the same, facing him with one of her legs tucked under her buttocks. He moved closer to her and she took his feet and put them across her lap. Anita said, "Get comfortable." Chris reached in his pocket and took out his smoke. He reached for the book on her table and she opened the drawer at the bottom and pulled a tray out for him with brand new paraphernalia. He said, "I thought you didn't smoke." "I don't, but you do. I keep this around in case I'd ever have a visitor that does. As you can see, you will be the first to use it." He started to question her but cleared his throat. "I have a feeling you got this just in case I ever came to visit." She seemed too perfect. What did she have up her sleeve? But deep inside, he knew she was the type to want to please her man. I've got to take it slow. "Nita, are you sure you don't mind?" "Not at all." She even had a bong/pipe, etc., but it was brand new; no wedding ring, no pictures of men, no ashtrays. He asked to use the bathroom, no signs of a man. He peeped into the bedroom, a nice big bed. Perfume on the dresser, no men's cologne, her closet open, a pair of pumps up against the nightstand, and no men's clothes in the closet—her decorations were that of a woman with a little masculinity. When he got back to the living room, she was still sitting in the same position. He felt skeptical and started to question her, but for some reason, he just knew he could trust her. She looked at him and said, "Chris, don't get the wrong idea. I haven't had company in years. I had a Tupperware party here for a co-worker, but that's all. I promise you can feel safe and never have to worry about anything here but love and affection. Ask me anything and I will be completely honest with you." Chris started to feel a little easier. She never took her eyes off him when she was talking. When he sat down, this time, he put his head in her lap. "Mmm." He could feel her heartbeat against her chest. One thing about Chris is he knew things about people. She looked into his eyes and he could see that she was sincere. He smoked a little and curled up in her lap and it felt too good he actually fell asleep in her lap. When he woke up, he was covered up with a blanket, the furry one that was on the back of the couch, and Anita was asleep also. He woke her up and looked at his watch. He had slept three hours and still in one piece. He looked at her again and asked her to scoot down on the couch. She did and reached up to put him in her arms. He looked over at the front door. "Chris, relax, everything is locked up. The security code is . . ." Then she got up off the couch. "Maybe I should be cautious of you too." She got up and took him on a tour of the place. Yeah, she had been a single lonely female, hard worker, looking for Mr. Good Bar and he knew that was him. She led Chris back to the living room. They got on the chaise lounge and covered up. He reached for the remote and Anita moved in close to Chris. He shook his head, "Girl, if you don't back up . . . we might end up doing something." Anita laughed and took him in her arms. "And don't you want to get to know me better?" He answered, "Shit! More than you know." When the television came on, it was on a gospel channel and the minister said, "Whatever you're doing right now must be in God's plan. Shall we bow our heads and pray?" They looked at each other and did just that. Chris curled up next to her, put his head in her chest, and they kissed for so long. Their bodies collided in rhythm to the kiss of the century. He found himself on top of her and he said, "Anita, don't do that." His breath was shallow. "Don't do what?" She had her tongue in his ear and let it move down to his neck. She stopped. "I'm sorry. It's been so long." She held him closer and kissed him slowly while they snuggled and talked for hours and kissed for more. They could hardly stand it, but as the night rolled on, they cuddled in each other's arms and fell asleep. They woke up in the middle of the morning and hugged and kissed some more, then went back to sleep. He woke up to the smell of breakfast at 4 am. They kissed and played around some, ate breakfast, fresh fruit, eggs, toast, chicken, fried steak, and juice. Anita fed him a little then put some fresh fruit in his mouth and kissed him as she sucked the juice from his lips and tongue and shared another kiss. Chris cleared his throat. She can cook too. "What time do you have to be at work?" he asks her. "I'm working from home today. Need to finish my book. I know you have to leave." "Not necessarily." Chris shook his head while staring at her, "I want to see what you were going to show me yesterday." "Okay." She looked back at him while putting the dishes in the dishwasher. Anita pointed to her laptop on the kitchen table at the unfinished manuscript. "Whichever you prefer, you can just scan thru it, and read it whenever you have time. I printed one for you on the living room table." He went to the laptop and read the title. He laughed just as she expected he would. "Can I read this later?" "Sure. Hopefully, while you're sitting next to me. I made a duplicate copy of the photo album for you. It's not finished, but I would be interested to hear what you have to say." She pointed to the photo album, pictures of him in concert, and others. He had seen a few posted on social media, but none like these. They were photo art; they looked great. Chris eased his way to the kitchen counter where Anita was standing. He came up behind her and pressed her body against the kitchen sink. She leaned into him. They could feel each other's bodies. Chris ran his hands alongside her waist and thighs slowly and gently feeling every vibe she was giving him. Her body started to move with his. Christopher's tongue went in her mouth and he bites her bottom lip. She starts to hold Christopher even tighter. She found her hand getting ready to slide inside his pants, but she stopped herself as Anita started to tremble and her body went limp into Chris's arms as she climaxed just from the touch of him. Her panties were so wet. Christopher held her and kissed her some more. She turned around to kiss him back. They decided it would be a good idea to continue later. Chris left reluctantly looking back at her as she smiled. He said, "I'm going to work." Anita walked over to Chris. She wanted to submerge her body with his in making love all day and night, but they kissed goodbye instead. But when he got outside, he turned around and went back, She was waiting for him. She took him in her arms as soon as he walked back on the porch. They spent the day together. He took her for a ride on his bike. It felt so damn good to hold him while riding on his bike. She pressed her body against him. When they got to a stoplight, they kissed again. Anita had to break the kiss. After all, she didn't want to use the beach bathroom. Luckily, she brought an extra pair of panties. They went back to the beach, the museum, and to the park for a picnic. Chris loved the way her body felt next to him on the bike, so damn warm. At the end of the evening, he drove her home, kissed her at the door, and started on the way home, although he didn't want to leave and she didn't want him to ever leave. They broke their embrace. He drove in silence with the music playing. He left the rose petals in a vase on the kitchen counter in a water-based solution. When Anita unlocked the door and went inside, the whole place smelled of roses. She went to the kitchen to see the rose petals floating on top of the vase. She picked it up and smelled it. The smell was divine. She picked up her phone to leave him a text message, but the number he called from read private. Then, when she looked on the fridge, Chris left the number there in big letters, "Don't leak my number." She texted him a single word, "Roses."

Chris made a few stops on the way home. By the time he got home, it was almost dark. The clicker was in the kitchen. He went around the side of the house and opened the door. When he went in, he opened the garage. He walked through the house to the garage and drove his bike inside. He took his jacket off and laid it across the couch. Damn. It was quiet and he felt free. He checked out his social media sites as we all do. He engaged in social pleasures one way or another. The time alone would give him a chance to think over the choices he had made in life. He liked this woman a lot and wanted her to be a part of his life. He could tell she didn't mind spending time alone, but would love to be with a man of her choice and her dreams—a woman who wants her man to know every inch of her, all the parts of her body. He could tell that she had been emotionally drained by the men in her past and that she was totally different. Her mind, body, and desires were only for one man, and he wanted to make sure it was him and only him. She seemed quiet and reserved but most of them do at first, then they change. But for some odd reason, when that church program was on, a feeling came over his entire body and he felt at home. "I can't get her off my mind. Let me go take a shower." Chris walked around the house. He was used to having a lot of people around but wanted to spend some time alone to review some business deals and his private life. How would she feel if there was a house full of people all the time regardless of their position? And where they fit in, everybody had a certain job. Would she fit or would she be reluctant? He didn't really like to be alone, but for some reason, this time, it felt good. Chris went to his room, took off his clothes, and went to the shower. He heard his phone on the ride home but didn't answer.

He thought about her more and more. This behavior was new to him as far as not just wanting sex. He was developing an emotional attachment. Maybe he'd call her later. Before he got home, he checked the text and when he got to a stoplight, it said roses. Chris thought about the message again as he walked naked to the shower. He left his bedroom and walked to the hallway bathroom. The hallway was dim and quiet. He preferred to use the one in the hallway as opposed to the one in the master bedroom, but the one in the hallway was always full of guests or people who lived there. He had asked everyone to find their own spot elsewhere. Chris turned on the water. He liked it warm. He stepped in and the water covered his head. The water ran from his head to toe, beating against his chest. Chris closed his eyes and envisioned her standing next to him in the shower, water pouring all over her body, trickling down her breast, and making a path to her vagina where he would put his hand while sticking his tongue in her mouth for her to suck on his fingers. The water dripping down their faces, she bends down and takes his love stick in her hands, then teases his abdomen and navel. Her lips and tongue start to tease him making a road map of his penis, getting to know it with her mouth. She treats it like she would his heart—with the utmost care, getting to know it better, becoming one with it. She wanted to know where he would receive the most pleasure and which part of him was the most sensitive. She was looking in his eyes. When he leaned his head back, she used her tongue teasing the head, kissing, sucking, tasting him like it was the only meal she would get in a long time. He massaged his hands through her hair gently. She pulled him down to her, the water making circles around her areolas. They were big, soft, brown, and sweet. Hmmm. Chris felt himself getting an erection. He wanted to know. Would she be the aggressor or would he have to be aggressive with Anita? She looks like she knows how to please a man from head to toe. The two days he had with her were different, more than he had ever spent with any woman. He felt like they had made love. They didn't make love but came close to it several times. It was more time with her that he looked forward to. Meeting Anita was a dream come true, his future, his desire, his new beginning. And her everlasting love, until next time.

Win love, lose love, choose love, and never choose to be undecided again.

Anita Johnson Brown.

Solid Gold Love* After Midnight

The alarm clock was going off. Chris opened one eye and looked at Anita. Usually, Anita was the one to turn it off. Chris reached over Anita and hit the off button. Rubbing his body against hers, she moved around and reached for Chris. She was half asleep but wanted to make love to Chris. On most mornings, he was her alarm clock. He would wake her up with his warm kiss, touching her in places that only he knew would make her moan his name. In deep ecstasy was where he led her always. When Chris and Anita went on their second date, he never thought things would end up the way they did. Find out what happens in The After Dark Files of Chris and Anita Brown.

Anita must have known they would have something special because when Chris walked in the door, she turned around and gave him a kiss. It was long and sweet. Her tongue danced in his mouth. It touched his inner soul. He put his arms around her and held her tight. As they walked to the living room still holding each other, her nose caught the sweet smell of roses. She went to the kitchen, made a pot of coffee, and took out the fresh chocolate cupcakes with fudge icing. She said, "Hey babe!" Her voice sounded so soft, delicate, and sexy before she even knew it. She wondered if it was too soon to call him babe. It was done. "Would you like coffee and a sweet snack?" "Wait, baby, I'm on my way to the bathroom." Chris went to the bathroom with a smile on his face, "Damn, we called each other babe and baby. I don't know where this is going, but damn, I sure don't wanna go home tonight." Chris washed his hands and noticed a picture of him sitting on the countertop in the bathroom. He picked it up. It was the one with him that had no shirt and a towel wrapped around his waist, and the bulge sticking out from the towel was a sight to drool over. He put the picture frame back down and thought to himself, "Yeah, that's my baby, and if she kisses me one more time like that, Imma marry her. Yeah, my Anita girl." Chris walked out of the bathroom. He passed by the bedroom on his way back to the living room. He didn't see her. He called out her name, "Anita, Nita," and she responded by saying, "I'm in here Chris, in the bedroom." He thought, "I just passed by there, why didn't you stop me? I was changing into this. What?" He said, "This." She stood there, a vision of loveliness. She wore a long, red appetizing piece of designer lingerie that fit every inch of her thick, curvy body. He got an instant erection that she couldn't take her eyes off of. She opened the side showing her legs and thighs. The split showed her panties. They were decorated with roses all over them. She walked closer to him and led Chris back to the bathroom. They stood in the mirror. She turned him around and said, "Chris, I want to make love to you and I know it's too soon and this is only our second date, but I want you so bad. I want to show you what it feels like when a woman desires a man as much as I desire you, how good it feels." Anita started to undress Chris, taking off his sweatshirt. His chest was just the way she liked, smooth, with tattoos, and she kissed his chest and didn't miss an inch. Her tongue was warm and wet. He reached for her and she said, "Not yet, babe, I want you to feel me, know me intimately. I want to give you the desires of a king. Let me run us a bath with the rose water you made for me the other day." And she turned on the water, testing the temperature and asking Chris if it was just right. Then, she pulled the stopper up. As the tub filled with water, she kissed him softly and gently, sucking his bottom lip and then letting him suck her wanting tongue. Her hands moved to release the enormous swollen man muscle protruding between his legs. It was as though they were hypnotized in the view of each other, and then he undressed Anita. Their naked bodies made a flame. When they got in the tub, the smoking heat engulfed their bodies and the smoke from the heat set a blaze of burning love's desire. Her skin looked golden and his looked brass, and they made sweet, gentle love. He picked her up and was inside her. They were like animals in the wild, screaming, biting, rocking their bodies. They only looked up once to see the moonlight cascading in the window, and he whispered, "I love you, Anita." And she whispered, "I love you, too, Christopher." They climaxed together, leaving each other in a pure sea of love. They laid in the tub in each other's arms talking, kissing, and wanting to make love again. They washed each other and when Chris washed her sweet rose petal, she spilled her liquid and called out his name. Once she was able to recover from all that love, she led Chris to the bedroom. Chris spread himself out on the bed and Anita first made love to Chris with her tongue and lips covering every spot on his body, knowing and discovering every part of his sensitivity. She bathed him with her tongue and made sweet love to him all night long. Her lovemaking is like a song that he will always think about when they make love, but knowing her, she will give him a new song every night. He felt a little uneasy because he wanted this to last. Anita is an everlasting love, and to the dick heads that let her go, audios bitch! She is all mine. Anita fell asleep in his arms. He was still inside her, feeling her squeeze her vaginal muscles clamping him down, letting him know she loves the way he made her feel and wanted him to stay inside her all night. He felt his body tingle every time she would squeeze his penis. He started to throb and she woke up looking in his eyes. She squeezed and he pushed deep inside her. She moaned and whispered his name, "Christopher, I want you again. What time do you have to work? I can get up and make breakfast for you babe, but to be honest, I can stay in this position with you inside me all day. He seemed speechless and said, "Well! Let me make a few calls. I might be able to just go in late. My schedule is hectic, but I promise I will be back tonight. Let's say around eight pm." "What would you like for dinner?" "Chicken or tacos, or you can bring me lunch. I'll leave the address and phone number on the nightstand, but for right now, let's make love till the sun comes all the way up." Once they started to explore each other again, moving to a rhythm so smoothly like the dance of love, Chris nibbled on Anita's ear and she arched her body calling out Christopher's name. He said, "Wait, baby, Imma call in, just this once. I have to go to the studio later for a few hours." And Anita said, "Okay." When Chris made his call, she moved her body on top of his while he was on the phone, just squeezing him and he was closing his eyes in ecstasy. They made love for hours.

Chris was still inside her when he woke up. Again, the sun was shining through the curtains. He missed several calls on his cell. He looked at her and kissed her lips. "Let's see where this goes. I'm sure Anita feels the same way." She moved around and said, "Chris, I love you," never taking her eyes off his. Her body felt so warm, plush, and soft like the duck-down pillow under his head. Anita had Chris mesmerized and Chris had Anita intrigued and spellbound. They shared an intimate kiss as they showered together, then made breakfast, feeding each other, giggling, smooching, and teasing one another. It was five o'clock and they made love again. After his shower, Chris got dressed and went to the studio. He was there for six hours, working his ass off. Before he left, Anita gave him a key, the one to her heart and to her home. He thought about her at the studio and wrote another song in addition to the one they were working on. An hour later, he was riding his chopper back to the woman he couldn't get enough of. When Chris pulled into the driveway, the light was on in the living room. He put the key in the door. The house was warm. He smelled the roasted chicken, potato hash, and roasted asparagus spears she made. Anita was curled up on the couch with her laptop. She heard him come in the door. He walked over to her. Anita reached for Chris. Damn! "I'm glad to see you." She smiled, "I was afraid you might stay at the studio or go home. You can stay here. Now, come let me rub your back and feed you." They ate dinner, talked, took a long lovemaking shower, and Anita massaged his body all over with warm oil, seducing Chris even more. They made love again and again for hours, touching, exploring, and feeling each other's bodies. Anita fell asleep and he held her. It felt like heaven on earth. Chris looked over at Anita. She was sleeping peacefully, like a baby, and he was about to do the same. He fell asleep in her arms.

Until next time. Hope you enjoyed part 2 of **After Dark.**

Solid Gold Love* After Midnight

The After Dark Series, from the Romance files of Chris and Anita Brown. This book will set your most intimate desires on fire. Look for the Novel on Amazon Kindle. It will be an extended version. Also, look for our Children's book series, starting with Walla Walla Woo Cat, The Relationship Guide; Rose of Desire, and The Golden Treasure, all on Amazon Kindle, in paperback and e-book.

Written by Anita Johnson Brown

Brand: Chris and Anita Brown

Lead Me on or Lead Me Home

In each other's arms is where they felt safe and warm with no problems crossing their minds. The connection between the two of them was so strong it was alarming. Did they fall for each other too soon? Chris looked at Anita while she was still sleeping. Her lace panties were still pulled to the side and her sexy lingerie was tucked underneath her behind. He wanted to pull it from underneath her body but she was sleeping like a baby. He leaned over and kissed her and she moves her arms inching closer to Chris. His body reacted and he pressed himself against her. The softness of her body against his was soothing.

Chris closed his eyes and moaned her name, "Hmmm, Anita." She moved even closer and placed her legs on top of his. Her breast pressed against his chest and he caressed her arm. Anita raised up one elbow. Her sleepy eyes centered on him as if nothing else mattered in the world. He had mixed feelings, not about himself, and the way he was feeling or maybe he did. The feeling was about the way Anita felt—was she leading him on or leading him home? It felt so good to have her next to him and when she moved her body on top of his, all confusion evaporated his thoughts and he became a master of seduction, love, and overjoyed affection and the only thing he saw in her eyes was that she loves him. Would she be able to withstand his lifestyle? An entertainer and an artist have a strange way of life. Sometimes, seclusion slips in and anger comes out and for no reason, maybe due to the demand. Wanting to be alone is a short span, but it does occur. Sometimes, bitterness and wanting to be around a lot of people is an avenue of letting go of anxiety and stress, and sometimes, not caring about their erratic behavior comes up every blue moon. Some life adjustments need to be made. But as he watched her climb on top of his body, it seemed as if she would understand his every move. Would she define him as obsessed if he wanted her to be with him all the time or would he change for the woman he loves? When they talked, she had the same intentions as him. Real love is very hard to determine but at the same time, they both said, "I love you," and the world and time stood still. He could feel the words penetrate through his body. Every bone, organ, blood vessel, and muscle in his body reacted. He could feel the blood flow through every artery and vein. He could feel the clean oxygen come in and the poison of carbon leave his body. His mind was fixed on her, and he knew they would be together like a match made only in heaven. It was the first time Chris said "I love you" to a woman and knew it may last forever. It wasn't forced; it was happening naturally. Anita made love to him while he laid there with only the feeling of total pleasure seeping through his body. Chris started to fall asleep. She kissed him and he reached for her. She whispered, "Babe, I'm going to take a shower and make you breakfast. I know you have to work or you can work from here. I can set up a place for you in my studio, or you can use the spare bedroom. It's up to you. I'm not trying to be pushy, just giving you some options." He smiled and said, "Come back to bed." And she looked at him and smiled, "Only if you insist," and she fell in his arms. Anita looked at him and said, "Chris, I think we are on the same page. I am the other part of your soul and you are mine. I understand what you require and desire. I just ask that you be completely honest with me and when you need time alone, let me know. And if you don't, then I am thrilled with knowing that. When you want me, I am here. You laughed when I told you how many years it had been since I've had sex with anyone. Six years and then you came into my life and I could not deny or resist you. And I prayed about it, so I know it's right, and you are falling asleep on me so let me lie here in your arms and we can melt into a ball of togetherness because there is nowhere else I'd rather be than right here with you Christopher." They fell asleep till noon, waking up to a small storm of thunder and lighting. Chris got up and opened the curtains, so they could lay and watch mother nature, and Anita welcomed him back to bed.

Anita looked at Chris and she wondered if he was leading her on or if she was his heart's desire. She felt uneasy but totally in love with Chris. Was it too soon? Would she scare him away or was this a match made in heaven? She was leading him home. All night long, they made love for hours. It started to rain just a little. The water hitting against the window made the sound of music. They talked and it seemed like they knew each other all their lives.

Until next time. We hope you enjoyed the After Dark files of Chris and Anita Brown, Lead me On or Lead Me Home. Written by Anita Johnson Brown.

Brand-Chris and Anita Brown

Rose of Desire*Strange Love

Chris has a desire greater than the need to survive his everyday life. He wanted her like he wanted to see the sunrise every morning and to gaze his eyes on the moon and the stars at night. And his need is not just a dream. He craved to lay in her arms all night and feel the pressure of Anita's body against his. He needed to feel her love every day, and not just sexually. If it was the last thing he did in life, he would make her his, his obsession, his only love, his wife.

He wanted her more than anything in his life. He craved her smell and wondered what she would taste like, what her body would feel like in his arms. The water dripped down his spine, never hitting his body the same way. He felt his penis rise to the occasion just thinking about Anita, her thick curvy body, her long, curly hair, tight-fitting jeans with a fancy classy blouse, and her lips painted ruby red. He found himself stroking his rod in the shower. Chris imagined her sitting on his face, her vagina lips fat and swollen, juice running over his beard, his tongue moving back and forth against her love button. When Chris thought about bringing Anita to a screaming climax, he exploded. His breath was shallow and hard. Chris finished his shower, wrapped a towel around his waist, and brushed his teeth. He oiled his body with Ralph Lauren. He could still feel the chills running up and down his spine as he thought about Anita and her soft hands rubbing the oil over his body. Chris dressed in a white tee-shirt and shorts. He could still feel the steam and warmth of the shower. He unlocked the door to the bathroom. The mirror was still full of steam. Damn! She was still on his mind. Was he thinking clear? No woman had ever made him feel this way. Consumed with thoughts of Anita Brown, he started to drift into an intimate memory. He enjoyed the ride so much. "Guide me that I may approach her in the right way and forgive me if I don't. She is my deep burning desire and the captive of my soul."

"All I have been through for so many years, and I'm still here. I need you, Anita. I want you. I have to have you, my angel. You are the reason I get up in the morning. I watch you every day." Chris admired her from afar and near. He made long trips just to see her and watch her every move, and when they saw each other, she would smile at him and he would rise to the occasion. They would just stare at each other. He decided to buy a house in the city she lived in to be near her. Anita teased him and he teases her. As his thoughts got more mystifying, he found himself downstairs. The coffee pot had just signaled the brewer was finished. He picked up his favorite red cup and poured his strong black coffee with just a touch of sugar. Chris picked up his Rolex off the kitchen counter and checked the time. It was almost 8:00 am. Anita would be leaving for work. He picked up his BP sweatshirt, zipped it up, and put the hoodie on his head. As he walked toward the front door, his dog followed him. From the front door and across the fence, he could see her. She looked so damn good, thick, and sexy—not at all a little girl but a full-grown woman. When she approached her car, her walk was so sexy. She threw her hips like a lady needing a man to sculpt her, a pure statue of love. The wind blew just a little and Chris stood watching her. The wind carried a whiff of her perfume right in his nostrils. The essence of her smell made him rise again and his heart pounded, beating like drums. His thoughts of her embedded within his mind, body, and soul. Just the smell of her scent, her intoxicating perfume, almost drove him to orgasm. Just when she looked up, he stepped back. Would Anita think it was odd that he would want her so much that he would go through any length to get her? Just the thought of her being with another man would drive him crazy. He had waited long enough. He knew her inside out, her every move, and desire. "I can make her a very happy woman in every aspect. Will she accept my strange ways? My insatiable need to have her with me day and night, wanting to keep her to myself, not sharing her unless of course, it's with our children," he thought to himself. She unlocked her door and got in the car. Before she drove off, she looked his way, "Damn! Did she see me? No more of this game of chase the cat. I know she goes to the store at night, hates the crowds, or should I go to the gas station she goes to, or maybe the tire shop? One way or another, I need to strike up a conversation. What if I get hard while I'm talking to her?" He just smiled to himself, went back into the house, and headed to the studio. He took a seat at the console. How would he start the conversation? He was undecided.

Anita was intrigued by him. She loved the way he looked at her, always just a step away from that tip-of-your-tongue conversation.

She got in the car, pulled her skirt down, and unbuttoned her jacket. She loved to dress in business attire. Her medium leather-heel pumps were just right for the office. She started the engine of her BMW. It was her favorite type of car. That engine purred like a kitten and the sound system made her body move with desire thinking about him. She put in his CD and enjoyed the ride. He was driving her crazy. Her thoughts of him at night drove her into multiple orgasms. She would be soaked even in her sleep. She would wake up to a satisfying climax, unable to utter a word, just a moan and an earthshattering body convulsion of pure ecstasy. She got wet while driving. Too bad she couldn't pull over and take care of the situation. When Anita pulled into the parking lot at work, she reached into her bag to make sure she had a fresh pair of panties. She turned off the ignition, stepped out of the car, and heard the automatic lock and alarm come on, still thinking of Christopher Brown. When she climaxed, she would say "Oh! Christopher. Damn, Chris, I want to invite you over to dinner." How would she ask him? Would he even be interested in a woman like me? I haven't had a man in years and my body is craving him, wanting him. One thing about me is when I give my love to you, you will be the only man who can light my fire, ignite my soul, and captivate my mind. He would be blessed to have a woman like me, and I'm nothing like his previous escapades. I know if he gets to know me, we would fall madly in love. We would be inseparable, non-divided, like Siamese twins, an amazing couple with so much to offer the world. I would be his better half, the true missing rib to his body, his soul mate, and defiantly his official wife— Anita, a one-of-a-kind woman. She thought about him more as her hips swayed from side to side gliding like a ballet dancer in rhythm into the office. She went to the ladies room. In the stall, she put a protective sheet on the stool before taking a seat. As she pulled her black lace panties down, they were soaked. She wanted to touch herself so damn bad but you never know. What if they have hidden cameras? She wiped herself with scented toilets in her purse and dried her half-shaved vagina with a clean, soft cloth she carried in her purse, still thinking of him. She put the cloth in the small Gucci coin bag and slipped the red Victoria's Secret panties on. She could imagine Chris taking them off of her slowly and kissing every spot on her body. Anita looked down at her watch. It was almost 9:00 a.m. She had to be at her desk to write an article due at 10:30 am. Anita washed her hands and dried them then dabbed a small amount of her favorite Chanel Mademoiselle on her neck and upper thighs, checked her hair and lipstick, buttoned her jacket, made sure her skirt was just right, and swayed to her desk. When she sat down, she noticed she left her black panties in the restroom. Anita locked her purse in her desk drawer and went to the restroom to get them. As she was walking down the hall to the ladies room, Gerald, a co-worker much younger than her, spoke and tried to hug her. Sometimes, she would walk her to her car. He was very nice-looking and eyed her constantly. He was nice, polite, and flirty, but never asked her out or anything. They were just friends, but the ladies in the office and everywhere else would eye this handsome, light-skinned, curly-haired, muscle-toned young man. They said hello and went their separate ways. When she went into the stall, her panties were gone. "I checked the wastebasket and looked behind the toilet, no panties. Strange. As I walked back to my seat, I sat down in wonder and amazement. I unlocked the desk drawer and looked in my purse, and the Gucci coin purse was gone. What the hell." She called security to have the lock changed on her desk drawer. They sent someone right away. After the lock was changed, she was handed the keys by the security officer Lee Han. He didn't ask her to sign a report. He just looked at her and said, "No problem, Anita, just be careful."

Han walked away with a smile as he tucked the underwear deep inside his uniform pocket.

Anita thought to herself. Lee Han is nice but sort of weird in a nonchalant kind of way. She dismissed the thought and put her mind on her article. She finished it before 10:30 and had the messenger take it to proofing and then to print. Anita wondered if Chris was shy. Chris, shy? No! Not him, not the famous Chris Brown. When she said his name or heard his music or his voice, her body would tingle all over. She could hardly speak. What he did to her was more than she had ever imagined a man would ever do. "I want to know him better, every inch of him, how he feels, how he tastes, how sweet his kiss is, and how the warm blood flows through his blood. I desire the thrill of being his only woman and true love. Would he think I am odd because I ride solo? And I am picky. Some call me stuck up or that boujee ass bitch, but a humble one, a no-nonsense female, 100 percent woman, made for only one man. I gather these celebs like to have more than one female. I'm selfish in the love department and do not like to share my man. I want him all to myself. In wedlock, we shall become as one, making passionate love, traveling the world, sailing the sea of love, creating and sharing business ventures, and loving our four children."

I want to keep him so drained, making love to Christopher that he won't have time to even want another female. I love to please my man, by all means necessary, and as a grown woman.

I have been waiting for that door to open where I can pour my heart out to you, and only you. When I think of you, time stands still. You are there.

Strange Love

I can please him in every way possible. Who would know I haven't been with a man in so long?

Strange Love... Burning Desire

My need and desire are overwhelmed by the need to please others. That may be one of the reasons I went into nursing in high school. I got my first nursing kit when I was five or six years old. Pleasing your family is easy and expected, even with patients. With other people, it can be demanding. The need to please my man is simply a desire, making sure his every need is met, especially his state of emotions. His feelings are important and so is his body. I imagine this type of man has the need to be fed in every way possible. His needs may be overwhelming and I am the perfect woman to fit these uncommon desires. I am the perfect specimen to fill him up, mind, body, and soul. His desires run rapidly; his needs are many, ever-changing, and expanding. He needs to be guided by my inner emotions and knows that the needs of my body crave to be manipulated by him on a daily basis because he is the only man who will ever be able to please me in every way.

Back at Anita's Desk

When Anita left the bathroom, Lee Han went in with the janitor. Mr. Han had been stationed inside of the building. The other officers were stationed outside of the back and front of the building. Cameras were everywhere. The Brommorilly Marketing Firm was tightly secured. Mr. Brommorilly was a seventy-year-old millionaire. He was married to his wife Silvia, a tall, thin, twenty-two-year-old model who was sleeping with one of his security officers. She went through the male staff like she was accepting applications. All of the guards knew what her vagina was like. All of the men guards had a taste of Mrs. Brommorilly and I assume they wanted more of her. Her short, tight skirts and tight-fitting blouses were definitely not appropriate for the office but everyone turned their head to the idea of saying a word. She went through men like underwear and a few of the females. Holland Brommorilly had the same staff for years. The only way out of this firm was if you died. He employed 62 people and every year, he gave them a raise and a bonus, usually during Christmas and New Year's. He never failed to make us want to keep our jobs, and we did our best. Han was the only one who had not slept with Silvia. We knew that Holland knew but he turned the other cheek. This behavior served its purpose, but who knows? Strange love.

Han was not supposed to install cameras inside the bathroom stalls, but the entrance of the restroom and the sink area was always under security. However, it seemed like Han lived at the office. He was there all the time. Did he ever sleep? It was rumored that he was a wealthy man. He even had a small single apartment in the back of the security area. There were two guards who patrolled the inside of the building, but they were never in the face of the employees. They're very friendly with Silvia whenever she worked in the outer office.

With Han's job, he was the head of the security. Nothing got past his roving eye. He only left his post to inform the staff of any changes, new rules for safety measures. When he wasn't at his post, every part of the office was locked down. Han worked all the time. He installed hidden cameras in all the restroom stalls. When he saw Anita enter the restroom, he panned the camera in her direction. He started to get an erection immediately. He got up and locked the door to the entrance. His secretary Teri, a beautiful blond with short hair, thought of Han as a creep. He was smart at his job, the best at what he did, but he was a quiet pervert, peeking, creeping, a voyeur with not many words, straight to the point with no conversation or friendliness. They both worked for Holland since he opened the firm. She knew when he locked the door, he was up to something. Thank goodness he was not the least bit interested in her. She was married with five children. The last thing she wanted was for Han to look at her in any other way besides business. She looked at the clock on the wall. It was only noon. Her lunch was at 1:00 p.m. She would lock the security department or have lunch at her desk. With five children, you get used to fixing lunches, and making one for herself and her husband Manny was no problem. Besides, she saved the extra cash for the kids' college fund and expensive vacations, which were mandatory. The boss always gave them a bonus at vacation time. She loved the time alone with her family. During vacation time, the kids were very obedient. She thought she heard Han moaning. "What an ass wipe. He was probably watching porn or something." Teri put her headset on and the next thing she knew, he was walking out of the office. "Back in 30, Terr." She hated when he called her that. Under her breath, she said, "Sure, you don't want to take the rest of the day off." He let the door close behind himself locking. "Terr," he said as he was walking to the men's room, "if you weren't married to a political figure, I screw your brains out and then dump you, goody two-shoed bitch. I have my eyes on someone else." Han passed up the men's room and headed for the ladies room. He entered the stall after he announced himself. He was smooth and swift. She had left her panties in the stall. Han put them in his pants' pocket after he smelled them, his eyes closed. As he was leaving the stall, Han left the restroom and went back to his desk. He watched her as she walked down the hall back to the restroom. Her walk was that of a strong, black woman, one he had always dreamed about, but he dared to speak to her. He had a rule with a woman, his need to control her every move. He was single and the woman of his dreams was not anyone he had ever come into contact with. On a personal basis, it was her he dreamed of having. If not, then no one. He walked to her desk. None of the other co-workers were watching him. He unlocked the desk, reached for the Gucci small bag, and slipped it in his inside jacket. He locked the desk. He knew he would get a call from her when he returned to his office. He watched her open her desk. He waited and panned the area. The camera followed to the ladies' restroom. He watched Anita until she came out of the restroom. Back at her desk, she rummaged through her purse, and like clockwork, his beeper went off. She needed him at her desk. He waited five minutes and called her back. When she hung up, he smiled, took the sweet-smelling panties out of his pocket, and licked the center, guava and chamomile. They were still wet. Did she have someone? If she did, it would mess up his plans. Anyway, he didn't want to think about it. He turned the zoom feature off the cameras so he could see everybody.

Anita sat at her desk. Her mind was on Chris. She had just thought of a way she could strike up a conversation. She would look up his number doing a little research. They worked with celebs all the time. As she navigated through her directory system, there it was, his entire file. She would call him after lunch and see if he needed anything. She would, of course, tell him who she was. She had just made her own day. Anita thought why wait? She dialed from her computer. Chris didn't answer. She was disappointed but explained who she was and left a detailed message with her number at home and the office, hoping Chris would call her back. Anita started on another project.

Holland sat at his desk. He made plans to leave his wife. She was a cheater and a pure bitch, a money-hungry whore. And he was tired. Just as he was about to call Han, his phone rang. It was Chris. They talked and made a business deal. Holland told Chris he knew the right person for the job.

Holland wanted her to handle this one on a personal basis. She had to take the client to lunch and he needed her to have the plans ready. By the next day, he knew she was the only one who could come up with a marketing plan by the deadline. Holland hadn't seen Chris in a year. It would be great to see him.

Chris was just about to edit a video when his phone rang. He didn't answer; he had to finish. He already informed his assistant Antwan to let his fans know the video would be released that night before 8:00 p.m. He thought about her more, his Anita. He knew where she worked and decided he would do a little independent work for one of his clothing lines. He knew Holland and called the firm to set up a deal. He was going to ask for her, but Holland suggested her first.

This was his chance. Holland stated he had the perfect marketing agent to handle the job. The appointment was for the next day at 2.00 p.m.

Anita read over her agenda for the next day. She picked up the folder, giving her instructions of what Chris Brown expected. She already had in mind what she would present to Chris. She had been thinking of him and gathered so much extensive research that she could taste his aspirations. Her marketing plan was already prepared. All she had to do was present it to the man she was about to fall in love with. She knew it would happen if they spend time together. She thought about speaking to Holland, informing him that maybe she should give this project to another agent but then, how would she approach Chris? Maybe step on his foot in the market or bump into him on purpose. They had seen each other so many times. And she just wanted to walk up to him and put her arms around him, whisper in his ear, take him home, and cuddle up with him on the sofa, but he and his friend were together watching and teasing her saying, "Don't do it! She's going to kill you." The first thing she thought was that maybe he can't handle all this curvy loveliness, but his vibes were magnetic, pulling her heartstrings and making her heart pound faster as she swung her hips from side to side.

Walking down the aisle coming toward the frozen food section, I saw them and I smiled. There he was, the guy I had seen several times before, but he was always too busy to notice which is a shame because I could have been feeling his arms around me right now. His warm, vanilla-colored skin and gorgeous smile made my day. What a beautiful man for a pretty woman like me. After leaving the market, she thought of him daily and used her imagination nightly to submerge herself into a world untouched by anything but pure ecstasy, lying in bed thinking of Christopher Maurice Brown/Chris Brown and how it would feel for him to manipulate every part of her craving body. Only Chris Brown could solve the mystery of her desires.

Anita imagined him working his fingers and tongue inside her creamy, wet haven, tasting, licking, and working his fingers in and out of her wet mound while rubbing her breast. He put his fingers in her mouth so she could taste her sweetness. She engulfed her cherry-flavored liquid like she was in a desert of thirst. And he fell in love with the thoughts of her, that night, and all the next day, and every day after he could feel every vibe from her mind, body, and soul.

Chris knew he would go to any length to make Anita his only woman—a woman he could have all to himself, a woman who would enter a room and command attention, a beautiful, gentle woman inside and out, with a heart of gold, solid gold, and a woman he would make his wife. She is a woman he knew that no other celebrity could be with but Chris. She is like an untouched, delicate rose, saving her body for the man she loves, a woman whose petals need the attention and care that only Chris has the power to satisfy. In his community of friends, they would only wonder, imagine, and fantasize about what she was like, how she tastes, and how it felt to make love to her. They would always wonder why he was so involved in her every move, determined to have her with him every day. She is like a magic wand, a Jeanie in a bottle, a good luck charm, a special woman created by God as they all are, but this woman is beyond belief, a blessing to any man, but not every man can have her.

And I, Christopher Maurice Brown/Chris Brown, am the man she wants, needs, desires, craves, and can fulfill her every craving. If only other men knew the secrets of her womanhood and what it would feel like to be inside her, where not only our bodies meet but also our minds and souls become one with each other. They can marvel but never taste or would ever touch her. She is a woman without another man on her mind.

Anita is the woman of his dreams and his reality. He followed her again to the mall. The way she walks is a work of art, like an artist's masterpiece, and he promised to get her with no cap. And they are like a vine and cannot be without each other. During the pace and flow of her movement, there's never a misstep. He wished for her in every way. He could feel her as she walked. He knew that no other woman would be able to replace the gorgeous and beautiful Anita (Brown, her married name). When she saw Chris in the market, he was walking toward her smiling. Anita and Chris were both engaged in thoughts of each other and could feel their thoughts. He couldn't wait to see her the next day.

Anita's thoughts were interrupted by Han. He asked for the attention of all employees and gave out a verbal speech and a written notice to exit through the side door due to a new security procedure taking effect during business hours because they were interviewing in the security department. She took the notice and looked at his hand. She didn't pay attention earlier, but he had several scratches. Anita looked away, toward the reception desk, to avoid eye contact with Han. Han made her skin crawl. He took a second look at her before he left her desk. Anita wondered what was wrong with him but didn't give a shit, and instinct told her to stay away from him.

Anita read the notice, "Due to the change in security and hiring, all employees are instructed to please use side exit. The front and back of the office will be locked.

Thanks, Han

Head of Security"

The only thing Anita wanted to do was think about where she would take Chris Brown for lunch and clock out for the day to head home and take a hot shower. How happy she was. Holland chose her for such an important client, one she secretly loved. I have been waiting for that door to open where I can pour my heart out to you, and only you, Chris. When I think of your precious love, time stands still. Tomorrow is our day.

Until next time. This is a story from the Romance Files of Chris and Anita Brown, written by Anita Johnson Brown.